Vote for Cupcakes!

Also by Sheryl Berk and Carrie Berk

The Cupcake Club Series

Peace, Love, and Cupcakes

Recipe for Trouble

Winner Bakes All

Icing on the Cake

Baby Cakes

Royal Icing

Sugar and Spice

Sweet Victory

Bakers on Board

Fashion Academy Series

Fashion Academy

Runway Ready

Designer Drama

Vote for Cupcakes!

The Cupcake Club

Sheryl Berk and Carrie Berk

Published by Sourcebooks Jabberwocky, an imprint of Sourcebooks, Inc.
P.O. Box 4410, Naperville, Illinois 60567-4410
(630) 961-3900
Fax: (630) 961-2168
www.sourcebooks.com

Library of Congress Cataloging-in-Publication data is on file with the publisher.

Source of Production: Versa Press, East Peoria, Illinois, USA
Date of Production: August 2016
Run Number: 5007253

Printed and bound in the United States of America.
VP 10 9 8 7 6 5 4 3 2 1

To Papa Alan Berk:

You always have our vote for best grandpa.

Lead the Way

"What do you suppose ancient Rome would have looked like?" Mr. Gatlin asked the students in his fifth-grade history class at Weber Day School. "Put yourself right smack in the middle of 44 BC."

Delaney Noonan closed her eyes and tried to picture it. She saw lots of old buildings, fountains, courtyards, columns, and men walking around in white togas. Then her mind wandered off somewhere far, far away to a vision of a very modern Italy. She suddenly saw pizza, pasta, and Italian gelato—and those ooey, gooey mozzarella sticks she loved dipped in marinara sauce!

"Delaney?" The sound of Mr. G's voice made her eyes fly open. She was pretty sure he had heard her stomach growl.

"Sorry!" she replied, shaking off the daydream. "I spaced out there for a sec. I was thinking Roma Pizzeria—not ancient Rome. I could almost taste it!" She wiped a little drool out of the corner of her mouth.

"You haven't painted a single backdrop for the play," her teacher said, pointing to the blank roll of paper in front of her. "How is our class supposed to put on *Julius Caesar* with no Roman scenery?"

Delaney stared down at her paints and brush. "Well, how am I supposed to paint ancient Rome's aqueducts with no white paint?" she protested. "The only colors left are red and yellow—or orange if I mix them together."

"You could paint gladiator blood," Ryan, a boy in her class, suggested.

"Eww!" shrieked Sophie Spivac, Delaney's BFF at Weber. "That's disgusting."

"No, Ryan has a point," their teacher said. "Ancient Roman times were tough and filled with battles and bloodshed."

Delaney shrugged. "That still doesn't solve the problem of no more white paint," she insisted. She dramatically draped a hand over her brow. "I can't be expected to work under these conditions. It's so, so…amateur!"

"I'm sorry you feel that way," Mr. G said. "I thought you'd dive into the role of Caesar and be excited to help out with the sets."

"I am," she said halfheartedly. "I'm happy I got the lead in the play—but I'm afraid it's going to be awful." Mr. G frowned—he'd been working on the play with the class for weeks. But even he had to admit it was off to an awful start: there were no art supplies to create authentic sets, and the costumes were ridiculous.

"How am I supposed to play a Roman emperor in this?" she asked her teacher. She held up a green polka-dot bed-sheet that someone had donated. "You call this a toga?"

She pointed across the room at her friend Sophie, who was busy stitching her costume together. "And have you seen what Brutus's toga looks like? A sheet with pink kitties on it?"

Sophie nodded. "Brutus stabbed Caesar. He's not really the pink-kitty type."

Mr. G sighed. "I hear you, but there is nothing I can do about it. We have to make do. There's no more money in the school budget."

"Says who?" Delaney challenged him.

"Says the student council who decides where to allocate school funds," Mr. G explained. "This year, money went to the after-school soccer program…and the new computer lab…and the new flag hanging from the pole in the yard."

"But it's just not fair!" Delaney insisted. "Something has to be done!"

Mr. G handed her a flier. "Then do it," he said. "There's an election coming up for next semester's new student government officers. Why don't you run for fifth-grade president? Then you can fix all the things you don't think are fair in the school."

"Me?" Delaney stammered. "President?"

"I think you'd make an awesome class president!" Sophie exclaimed. "And I could be the First Friend."

"Think about it," Mr. G added. "Getting involved in student government is the best way to bring about positive change at Weber Day."

☆ ☮ ☆

That afternoon at the weekly meeting of Peace, Love, and Cupcakes, Delaney was having presidential daydreams while Kylie Carson, the club's president, went over the details of their upcoming orders.

"By the end of next week, we have to make eight hundred cupcakes for the Blakely Elementary School Winter Fest," she read out of her binder. "I told Principal Fontina it would be no problem. It helps if we stay on her good side."

The club's adviser, Herbie Dubois, nodded approvingly. He also taught Blakely's robotics class, and he had a knack for getting into trouble with the administration himself. Almost all of his inventions went up in smoke. The last one, something he called the Frost-inator, had exploded and left chocolate icing all over the walls and ceiling of the teachers' lounge. It took the club hours to clean it up.

"Did Principal Fontina give you any specifics?" he asked.

Kylie checked the order form. "Nope. She just wrote 'make them fabulous!' As if Peace, Love, and Cupcakes would do anything less."

She turned to her fellow cupcakers. "So what flavor would be wintry and wonderful?"

Lexi Poole's hand shot up. "How about gingerbread? Gingerbread men are my fave things to bake—next to cupcakes of course. I could make mini men on top of every cupcake with button eyes and bow ties made out of candy." Lexi was Peace, Love, and Cupcakes' resident artist and a whiz at making their sweets look special.

"That's a good idea," Kylie said, taking notes. "Any others?"

Sadie Harris, another one of the club's original members, piped up. "I think we should do sugar plum cupcakes," she said. "You know, like the Sugar Plum Fairy in *The Nutcracker* ballet?"

Kylie looked puzzled. Sadie was an expert on basketball—not ballet. "That's a cool idea too. Who knew you liked sugar plum fairies, Sadie?"

"I saw *The Nutcracker* at the New York City Ballet over Christmas with my grandma," Sadie replied. "At first, I thought I'd be bored. But it was pretty cool. That fairy had some moves. I'd like to go up against her on a b-ball court! Just not on my toes…"

Kylie giggled. "Okay, any other suggestions?"

Jenna Medina closed her eyes tight and smacked her lips together. When it came to baking, she had the golden taste buds. "Candy cane cupcakes," she said confidently. "With peppermint buttercream frosting."

"Yes!" Kylie exclaimed. "That's perfect!" The rest of the girls all nodded in agreement.

"I could do white chocolate skates on top," Lexi added, pulling out her sketchbook and colored pencils. "And sparkly blue snowflake sprinkles…oh, and mini candy canes, of course!" She drew a white cupcake with a swirl of white-and-red frosting on top. "How cool would this look?"

"*So* cool!" Sadie said approvingly. "And the display

6

needs to be cool too—literally. What about displaying the cupcakes on ice? Or having a giant snowman hold them?" Her dad was a contractor, and there was nothing Sadie could dream up that he couldn't construct.

"Love! Can you talk to your dad?" Kylie asked. "Ask him how we could build something snowy and keep it from melting."

"I can take a crack at it," Herbie volunteered. "Perhaps a little liquid nitrogen...or a hydrated artificial polymer?"

Kylie had no idea what Herbie was talking about, but he looked so eager to help. He always had an idea of how to "improve" PLC's cupcake baking, frosting, or display with an over-the-top invention. And while they all appreciated his enthusiasm and creativity, he didn't have the best track record.

"Maybe we should just leave it to the pros," she suggested. "Sadie's dad will know how to build it, no problem."

"But I could do it bigger and better—no offense to Sadie's dad."

Sadie shrugged. "None taken. Let's hear it, Herbie." Sadie was a real team player, a skill she'd picked up from competing expertly in every sport Blakely offered. "What are you thinking?"

Herbie borrowed Lexi's sketchbook to jot down a few calculations.

"I'm thinking of how they make snow at ski resorts back home in Canada," he explained. "They force water and pressured air through a 'snow cannon' of sorts."

Now it was Jenna's turn to speak up. "*Un momento, por favor*," she said. "You're saying you want to make a ski slope inside the Blakely gymnasium?"

Herbie scratched his head. "There must be a way to keep the snow contained so it only snows over the cupcakes."

"But won't the cupcakes get wet and soggy from the snow?" Kylie pointed out.

"Good point," Herbie said. "Let me think about it."

"Here," Lexi said, drawing a circle over his snow-making machine sketch. "We can make it like a giant snow globe so at least we won't get wet and soggy."

"Oh, that's awesome!" Kylie exclaimed. "Principal Fontina will flip out!"

"And that's a good thing?" Herbie asked her.

"I mean she'll love it," Kylie insisted. "Seriously, this could be our greatest display yet. Are we all in agreement?"

Sadie, Lexi, Jenna, and Herbie all nodded—but Delaney's

mind was elsewhere. As the girls all packed up, she sat staring into space.

"Laney?" Kylie poked her friend gently in the arm. "You awake in there? You didn't say a peep the entire meeting. Usually I can't get you to stop gabbing."

"Do you like being president?" Delaney suddenly blurted out.

Kylie had been the first to start the cupcake club at Blakely, and with the help of Jenna, Sadie, and Lexi had turned it into a booming baking business. When Delaney and Kylie met at sleepaway camp, Kylie had asked her to join the club—and now she was a full-fledged member of the team.

"Um, are you asking to take over my job?" Kylie replied nervously. "Did I do something wrong?"

"No, no, no!" Delaney reassured her. "You're a great president. I'm just asking if it's fun."

"Well, of course," Kylie said. "But it takes a lot of hard work and organization, and sometimes it's kinda stressful. Like when we have three orders due on the same day and I have to figure out how to get them baked, decorated, and delivered. Or when we have to come up with an idea that's never been done before."

She opened her binder to the recipe for Lemonade Laffy Taffy Cupcakes that PLC had made for Delaney's mom's baby shower.

"Remember these?" Kylie chuckled. "How we filled them with both blue and pink frosting to reveal your mom was having *both* a boy and a girl?"

Delaney sighed. "How could I forget? I passed out at the party! I was in shock!"

"Or these?" Kylie pointed to a recipe for applesauce mini cupcakes that they'd used to decorate a ball-gown skirt for a Cinderella-themed birthday party. "Remember how we had to roll you in wearing it?"

"I was the clumsiest fairy godmother," Delaney recalled. "I landed facedown on the floor in a puddle of purple frosting!"

"But the kids loved it," Kylie reminded her. "You sure know how to make an entrance!"

"I guess we've come up with a lot of amazing cupcakes, haven't we?" Delaney reflected. "And you like being president—even if it is a bit of a challenge at times?"

Kylie nodded. "Sure. Why?"

"No reason," Delaney replied, swinging her backpack over her shoulder. But Kylie knew when her friend had something on her mind. During the entire meeting, Delaney had had that faraway look in her eyes.

"Spill," she insisted. "What's up, Laney?"

"It's nothing…really," Delaney said. "No biggie."

"Then if it's no biggie, why can't you tell me?"

Delaney blushed. "You'll think it's silly."

Kylie pulled up a stool next to her friend. "I promise I won't."

Delaney stared down at her feet. "I'm thinking of maybe running for fifth-grade president."

"You?" Kylie gasped. She hadn't meant it to come out that way—but it was pretty startling.

"Yeah, *me*. What's wrong with that?" Delaney exclaimed. "You don't think I'd be a good one?"

"No! I mean, yes! You'd be a great one!" Kylie said. "It's just… Well, you've never really expressed an interest in politics."

"This isn't about politics. It's about paint. And sheets. And not having those little tater tots every Friday at lunch. I loved those tater tots and now they're gone!"

Kylie scratched her head. "You lost me."

"I don't like the decisions the student government has been making, and the only way to change them is to get elected president."

"Um, Laney, the president doesn't get to make all the decisions independently. I'm always asking you guys what you think. It's teamwork."

"Well, that's not the kind of president I wanna be," Delaney insisted. "I want to fix stuff."

"That's fine," Kylie tried to explain. "Fixing stuff is great. But you need to find out what the rest of your classmates think is broken too."

"Why?" Delaney asked. "I mean, isn't it obvious? They just need to listen to me." She pulled the flier out of her backpack. "Thanks, Kylie."

"For what?" her friend asked.

"For convincing me to run for president. I can't wait to get started campaigning!"

Kylie smiled but wondered if that really was the best idea—and if Delaney knew what she was getting herself into.

Promises, Promises

As soon as Delaney got home, she began working on her presidential posters. She wasn't quite the artist Lexi was, so she decided the best way to make a poster was to cut pictures out of magazines and glue them onto large poster boards. What was it her mom always said? A picture was worth a thousand words?

She rummaged through her family's recycling bin in the garage and found a bunch of magazines and newspapers. She ripped out any page that "spoke" to her: a photo of a delicious pepperoni pizza with gooey cheese dripping from a slice, a picture of a sparkly clean bathroom and a mop, and an ad for tater tots piping hot out of the oven.

She glued the pizza pic to a large red poster and wrote her first campaign promise above it: "Vote for Delaney if you want delicious school lunches!" She pasted the bathroom pic to a green board and wrote, "Delaney says no more messy girls' and boys' bathrooms!" Then she stuck the tater tots pic to a blue poster board and wrote in big, black bubble letters, "Delaney promises tater tots every Friday!" She stood back and admired her handiwork.

"What's all this?" her mom asked, finding her daughter sitting on the living room floor surrounded by piles of papers, scraps, and glue sticks.

"I'm running for Weber Day fifth-grade president," Delaney said proudly.

"Wow." Her mom's eyes grew wide. "That's great, honey. I had no idea you were interested in politics. Are you sure you have time? I mean with all your homework, the school play, your cupcake club…"

"I'll make time," Delaney insisted.

Her mom looked concerned. "Well, if you're sure you can handle it all…"

"It's really important," Delaney pleaded with her. "I want to make the school the best it can possibly be."

"Now that's a great campaign slogan," her mom said approvingly.

"It is, isn't it?" Delaney said proudly. She spied a giant letter *B* in a headline on the front page of the Sunday newspaper and snipped it out. Then she wrote on a piece of paper, "Vote for Delaney! Make Weber Day the best it can…" and triumphantly glued the letter *B* beneath it.

"Can we go to the copy store, Mom?" she asked. "So I can make a bunch of these to post around school?"

Her mom smiled. "I'm happy to help President Noonan in any way I can," she said and saluted her.

"I'm not president yet," Delaney reminded her. "But it would be great, wouldn't it?"

The next day at school, Delaney began plastering the hallways with the fliers and posters she had made. "Vote for Delaney for Prez!" she said cheerfully as she stuck one on Sophie's locker. It had a big picture of Delaney smiling and giving two thumbs-up. Around the words, she'd used gold star stickers.

"You're serious about this?" Sophie asked.

"Totally! And you have to help me…First Friend!"

She handed Sophie a stack of fliers. "Start handing these out and sticking them anywhere you see a blank wall."

"Here!" Sophie said, shoving one in her classmate Olivia Dante's face. "Vote for Delaney!"

Olivia wrinkled her nose. "What's this?"

Delaney stepped forward and cheerfully explained. "I'm running for fifth-grade president," she said, smiling. "Vote for Delaney!"

Olivia was short, with long, dark hair and dark eyes that always seemed lost in deep thought. Delaney noticed that she hardly ever smiled and was *very* serious in class, in gym, in chorus, in line in the cafeteria… Actually, she was serious all the time.

"Why should I?" Olivia asked, reading the flier. "I mean, what do you stand for?"

"Stand for?" Delaney replied. "What do you mean?"

"I mean, what are the important issues facing our school that you are going to address as president? Every candidate needs a platform."

Olivia pulled a flier out of her own bag. "Like this."

The sheet of paper read "Vote for Olivia for President" and had a long list of campaign promises: "I will ask for school to start five minutes later to allow for early-morning traffic. I will start a peer mediation program to help prevent bullying. I will meet with the administration weekly to discuss any and all student concerns."

"Wow." Delaney gulped. "This is really impressive. I

just wanted pizza for lunch every day and no more toilet paper stuck to the ceiling of the bathroom."

"Give me one good reason why *anyone* should vote for you over me," Olivia said.

"Because…well, because…" Delaney stammered. She couldn't think of a single reason—other than the tater tots—and she knew that was not as important as anything Olivia was proposing.

"Yeah, thought so," Olivia said. "That's gonna be a big problem in the debate."

"Debate?" Delaney was starting to feel a little queasy. No one had told her campaigning for class president was such hard work! "What debate?"

"The presidential debate Friday during assembly," Olivia said. "The candidates go head-to-head on all the issues and present their platforms to the student body."

"Did we know that?" Sophie whispered to her friend.

"We didn't…but it's not a problem," Delaney shot back. "I'll be ready."

Olivia shrugged. "I hope so—but this took me two weeks, and you've got just two days. Good luck with that!" She continued down the hall, handing out more fliers and campaign buttons that read "Liv Leads the Way 2 a Better Weber Day!"

"Not fair," Delaney said, sighing. "Nobody told me about this debate thing—or that I needed to make buttons."

"The debate will be a breeze for you," Sophie assured her. "You're a natural performer—you always get the lead in the school plays. If anyone can win over an audience, it's you."

"Acting is one thing," Delaney said. "But Olivia is smart. She really knows what she's talking about. I don't have a clue."

Sophie steered her toward the library. "Then figure it out. Do your research on successful presidential campaigns, and ask kids here in school what they think and want."

"That's kind of what Kylie said too," Delaney recalled. "About asking people's opinions."

"You want to be a great leader who represents the people—not a dictator," Sophie reminded her. "Remember where that got Caesar."

"With a huge Las Vegas hotel named after him?" Delaney joked.

"Dead!" Sophie exclaimed.

"Fine, I get the point. Talk to kids, get their opinions, and make lots of promises that sound better than Olivia's."

"Well, sorta," Sophie tried to warn her. "Just be careful not to make promises you can't keep."

But Delaney was already down the hall and out of earshot. She had a long, long list to write and a campaign strategy to plan.

When Delaney got to the library, Mr. G was at a table, surrounded by a mountain of books.

"Delaney," he said, smiling when he saw her enter. "I'm up to my eyeballs in ancient Rome, finalizing our script for the class play. Adapting Shakespeare isn't an easy task, but I need to make it clear and concise so everyone—even the younger kids in the school—understand. Care to join me?"

"Um, actually I need to be working on my political campaign," she said, trying to sound very official.

"So you're taking my advice and running for fifth-grade president!" he exclaimed. "Good for you. And history is an excellent place to start planning that campaign." He pushed out a chair and motioned for her to take a seat.

"You're lucky to be playing a great Roman general and statesman—it'll come in handy."

Delaney looked confused. "Caesar? I thought he was a bad guy? A bully?"

"He was a very popular leader and helped turn the Roman Republic into the powerful Roman Empire," Mr. G insisted. "He wasn't *all* bad. I find him fascinating."

"He's a great role to play—don't get me wrong," Delaney said. "But I'm not sure how that helps me run my campaign here at school."

Mr. G tapped his pen on the table. "Well, Caesar was a brilliant military leader, and his greatest talent was inspiring his troops."

"I don't have any troops." Delaney sighed.

"Ah, but you do! Your classmates. And they are looking to you for inspiration. What can you do to fire them up and get them on your side?"

"Fire them up? I dunno how," she said, shrugging.

"Well, what would Caesar do?" Mr. G asked.

"Um, he would ask his advisers for advice," Delaney recalled. "He had a really big posse: Brutus, Cassius, Marc Antony…"

Her teacher chuckled. "Yes, he most certainly did."

"Hmmm, I guess I could ask my most trusted advisers," Delaney said. Suddenly, she knew exactly what to do—and how to do it.

"Thanks, Mr. G," she said, grabbing her bag and rushing off. "I got this."

"I have no doubt you do!" he called after her.

Council Is in Session

Delaney insisted that the cupcake club meet after school at her house to start working on the Winter Fest cupcakes. They rotated volunteering their kitchens to bake orders, and it was supposed to be Sadie's turn—but Delaney convinced everyone that her mom needed her to help look after her twin baby brother and sister.

"Thanks," she said as they came through the door with bags of ingredients to start baking. "Tristan and Charlotte are big trouble for two little babies."

She ushered them into the kitchen and told them to each take a seat on a stool. "I have something serious to discuss," she said.

Kylie rolled her eyes. "Delaney, is this about running for class prez?"

"Shhh!" Delaney hushed her. She tried to remember some of what Mr. G had taught them about ancient Roman politics and recalled a speech he'd read them—something about friends, Romans, and countrymen…

"Friends, bakers, cupcakers…" she began. "Lend me your ears!"

She filled them all in on the lack of paint and proper togas, Olivia's campaign, and Mr. G's suggestions.

"Lemme get this straight," Jenna said with a sigh. "We go to Blakely and you go to Weber Day, but you want us to help you inspire two hundred kids at your school…*how*?"

"That's what I'm asking *you*!" Delaney said. "It doesn't matter if we go to different schools. You guys are my most trusted advisers. Help me inspire them."

"Inspire them to do what?" Lexi asked.

"Pick me," Delaney answered. "Make me their leader."

"It sounds like you need a pep rally, like before a game," Sadie piped up. "You know, cheerleaders and a bonfire and someone yelling 'Go, Delaney, go!' in a megaphone?"

Delaney wrinkled her nose. "It sounds a little too sporty for a presidential debate. But I like the part about chanting my name. That's very pop star."

Kylie wasn't thrilled that Delaney had ambushed the meeting, but she could tell her friend really needed help.

"You should do something that will make them remember you," she spoke up. "A logo or a campaign slogan, like the 'Hillary for America' bumper sticker my mom has on her car."

"Hmmm," Delaney considered. "'Delaney for America.' It has a nice ring to it."

"You need something more original—more you," Jenna added. "Like 'Vote for Zany Delaney!'"

Sadie cracked up. "Well, that's definitely *you*, Laney," she said. "Your Instagram post this morning with the fruit on your head was pretty out there!"

"I was feeling like a smoothie," she explained.

"It fits—but I'm not sure how the message 'Zany Delaney' will inspire kids to vote for you," Lexi said. She took out her sketchbook and made a few doodles. "What do you think?" she asked, holding up a page. On it, she had drawn a giant cupcake and written the words "A Sweet Thought: Vote for Delaney!"

"It's a good idea, but I think we can add some Roman military strategy to it," Delaney said, thinking out loud. "I remember from my history homework that Caesar had his soldiers decorate their weapons so they would carry them proudly into battle."

"Weapons? I was talking about cupcakes," Lexi reminded her.

"I know! But what if we hand out cupcakes and lots of different toppings?" Delaney suggested. "Have the kids all decorate their own so they are proud of them—and happy to vote for me."

"DIY cupcakes," Sadie chimed in. "That's a great idea, Laney. When would we hand them out?"

"At the debate on Friday," Delaney said. "Yes! This is so much better than Olivia's ideas! I am *so* going to beat her!"

"Is that why you're running for president?" Kylie asked her. "So you can beat her? I thought you wanted to make positive changes at your school."

"That too," Delaney said. "But it would be awesome to watch Olivia lose when she was so sure she was going to win." She smiled at the thought. "Talk to me about flavors and decorations for *my* campaign cupcakes."

"The flavor has to be a crowd-pleaser," Jenna insisted. "Let's do our famous Black Bottom Cupcakes with cheese-cake baked inside. No one can say no to those."

"And we can hand out sprinkles, chocolate chips, gummy bears…you name it," Lexi said. "Everyone can make their own cupcake masterpiece."

Kylie held up her hands in a time-out gesture. "Guys, before we get too excited, remember we have the Blakely Winter Fest to cater. Baking for Delaney's debate would mean we have to make a thousand cupcakes in just two days."

"Well, this is more important than some dumb winter party," Delaney insisted. "Can't you just tell your principal we're busy—and we'll do it next time?"

"A promise is a promise," Kylie insisted. "I gave Principal Fontina our word, and that means something."

"It means you don't have time to help your BFF!" Delaney fired back. "That stinks, Kylie."

Kylie took a deep breath and tried to stay calm. She was furious at how selfish Delaney was behaving! What was wrong with her? Delaney knew better! She knew how important it was to keep Principal Fontina happy. Without her permission, PLC would have no teachers' lounge kitchen to meet in at Blakely. Still, Delaney was her BFF, and this obviously meant a lot to her…

"I didn't say I wouldn't help you," Kylie said softly. "I just said we're going to have to figure out how to get both orders done on time. I have a huge English paper due Friday morning too."

"And I have a basketball game tomorrow afternoon," Sadie added.

"See?" Kylie pointed out. "We've all got tons to do."

"Well, we can divide and conquer," Delaney said, pushing Kylie aside. "Lexi, Sadie, and you can do the Winter Fest cupcakes, and Jenna and I can work on my campaign cupcakes—and I'll text my friend Sophie and get her to come pitch in too." She began barking orders and preheating the oven. "Let's go! My mom can take us to the supermarket to buy the ingredients, and we can start baking as soon as we get back. If Caesar could conquer Gaul, we can conquer a thousand cupcakes!"

"Caesar?" Sadie asked. "As in the salad?"

Lexi chuckled. "She means Julius Caesar, the Roman dictator."

Delaney tossed an apron at her. "Time's a-wastin' and we need to start tastin'. Jenna, you're with me on shopping duty."

"Well, she *sounds* like a dictator," Jenna added. "Do this, do that…"

Kylie had never seen her friend behave this way. It was as if the power of being president was already going to Delaney's head, and she hadn't even won the election yet!

"Laney, I think you should hit Pause for a sec," Kylie said, trying to slow her friend down. "We need to make a grocery list, figure out what we need and how much..."

"No time for lists!" Delaney ignored her and ran off to help her mom bundle up the twins for the ride to the market.

"We were planning on starting the Winter Fest order anyway. We've gotten all those ingredients already," Lexi pointed out.

"I'll go with *la chica loca* to the market," Jenna said. "Someone needs to make sure she gets the right kind of chocolate chips."

Kylie still didn't like the sound of this. "Laney," she called after her. "Who's going to pay for all these ingredients for your campaign cupcakes?"

Delaney froze in her tracks. "What do you mean? Don't we have money in our PLC savings account?"

Kylie frowned. "Yes. The key word being 'PLC.' Delaney, these cupcakes aren't for an order. They're for you."

"And they'll be pricey," Jenna pointed out. "All those toppings, really good chocolate..."

"Well, I'm a member of PLC, so PLC should pay for them," Delaney said, waving her hand dismissively.

Kylie's mouth fell open. Delaney was not only bulldozing over her, but also asking the cupcake club to give up some of their hard-earned profits to bankroll her campaign!

Before she could say another word, Sadie spoke up. "Laney, that's not really fair, is it? I mean, we need every penny to grow the business."

"Well, I'll pay it back…when I win," Delaney assured them. "I'll get everyone at Weber Day to hire PLC for parties, birthdays, school dances, you name it. We'll have more business then we can handle."

"We already do," Kylie muttered under her breath. "Thanks to you."

She watched as Delaney skipped out of the kitchen, dragging Jenna behind her.

"*Adiós*," Jenna called over her shoulder to the girls. "Wish me *buena suerte*, good luck!"

Shop till You Drop

Delaney ran down the aisles of the supermarket pushing her twin siblings in the cart. They both giggled in delight as she zoomed past the cereal and pasta and headed for the dairy section.

"Take it easy," Jenna said, panting. "This isn't a race."

"Milk, eggs…" Delaney called out as she tossed several cartons and crates into the cart.

"Hey! *Cuidado!* Be careful!" Jenna warned her. "You don't want your eggs scrambled!"

"Honey? The baking powder, sugar, and cocoa powder are down here," Mrs. Noonan called from the next aisle over.

"Go!" Delaney said, giving Jenna a shove. "I'll get the vegetable oil."

When they got to the baking aisle, she allowed Jenna a mere three seconds to make a choice about the chocolate chips. "Semisweet or milk chocolate?" Jenna pondered.

Delaney pointed to her watch. "Tick-tock, tick-tock!"

"Fine," Jenna said, scooping up several packs of the semisweet. "Happy now?"

☆ ☮ ☆

By the time they got back to Delaney's house, Sophie had arrived to help out, and the girls already had several batches of the candy cane cupcakes in the oven.

"Has anyone spoken to Herbie?" Lexi asked. "Do we know how his giant snow globe is going?"

"I'm afraid to ask," Kylie said. "The lights on the third floor of the school were flickering all day, and I'm sure it has to do with what he's doing in the robotics lab."

"OMG, I didn't think about presentation," Delaney said, suddenly remembering. "I can't just hand out cupcakes at the debate in plain cardboard boxes!"

"And why not?" Jenna asked.

"Because I have to do something big and flashy. Maybe a giant American flag made out of cupcakes? Or a marching band?"

Kylie sighed. This was getting out of control. "Laney, this isn't the election for the president of the United

States! It's for Weber Day fifth-grade president. I think you're getting a little carried away."

"Am not!" Delaney felt her cheeks burn. "It's important to me. And it should be important to you if you're my friend."

"I *am* your friend," Kylie pleaded with her. "But I'm worried you're blowing this out of proportion."

"You just don't like anyone else to be a president," Delaney protested. "You don't want anyone else to have power."

"Laney! That's not true and you know it!" Kylie cried. Just then, her phone dinged with an email. "Uh-oh," she said, reading it. "Major 911 at Blakely. Herbie needs help. His snow machine went crazy, and now it's snowing all over the third floor!"

"I'll drive you girls you there," Mrs. Noonan volunteered when she heard the girls panicking. "Delaney, make sure you listen for your brother and sister. They're napping in their cribs after the ride you gave them at the market." She placed a baby monitor on the kitchen counter.

"Great, just great," Delaney said, pouting. "So now we have to stop what we're doing to help Herbie clean up the mess he made? I'm not going anywhere."

"Delaney!" Sadie said, looking shocked. "How can you abandon your team?"

"You can do what you want, Laney," Kylie said, getting her jacket. "I'm going to help Herbie. He's our adviser, and we stick together." The rest of the girls followed, leaving Delaney and Sophie in her kitchen.

"Now what?" Sophie asked. "We haven't even made the batter for your cupcakes and they left."

"Who needs any of them? I'll do it myself," Delaney said. She pulled out Kylie's binder and found the recipe for Black Bottom Cupcakes.

"Hand me the cream cheese," she told Sophie.

Sophie rummaged through all the paper bags of groceries but found no cream cheese. "I don't see it. Did you forget it?"

Delaney thought for a moment. She remembered grabbing the other items she needed in the dairy section, but no packages of cream cheese. Maybe Kylie was right that she should have written a shopping list. But she wasn't about to admit she'd made a mistake…

She went to the refrigerator and searched. "No cream cheese, but we have a lot of Greek yogurt," she said, finding two large containers. "This will have to do."

"Are you sure?" Sophie asked. "That's not what the recipe says."

"Sometimes you just gotta wing it," Delaney said. "We'll make it work."

Just then, she heard Charlotte and Tristan fidgeting upstairs on the baby monitor. "Ugh, if my baby brother and sister let me work!"

☆✌☆

When the girls arrived at Blakely, all the halls were pitch-dark. Kylie switched on the flashlight on her phone.

"Herbie?" she called. "Where are you?"

"Up here!" came a voice from up the stairs. "I think I blew all the fuses."

"I can fix that," Sadie said. "My dad showed me what to do when we blow a fuse and he's at work." She pointed Kylie's light toward the fuse box on the wall and flipped a few of the switches. All the lights came on.

"Yay, Sadie!" Lexi cheered.

"Thanks," Herbie called down. "Now I can see… although I'd rather not."

They climbed to the third-floor landing and opened the door to the robotics lab. When they peered inside, they saw soupy white foam all over the floor and Herbie standing knee deep in it. Next to him was a huge metal machine with a giant hose and fan attached. On the front was a barometer of sorts, and the arrow on it was spinning wildly.

"I think I overestimated the snow maker's pressurizer," he said.

"What on earth happened here?" Kylie exclaimed.

"One time, my little brother Manny put too much laundry detergent in the washing machine and it looked like this in our basement," Jenna said.

"It's kind of the same thing," Herbie explained. "I put in a little too much water and turned the cannon up a little too high."

"None of this is little!" Sadie exclaimed.

"How do we even clean this up?" Lexi asked. "It's like a bowl of snow soup up here!"

"Principal Fontina will freak," Kylie said. "And I don't mean that in a good way."

"We need a giant vacuum to suck it all up," Sadie said. "Either that or a really big straw."

"A vacuum is not a bad idea," Herbie said. "If I can reverse the pressurizer to draw in the snow instead of blowing it out, I think we'll be in business."

He fiddled with the machine, making a few adjustments with a wrench and a screwdriver. "Stand back, everyone," he said. "This will either be a huge success…"

"Or an epic fail," Kylie said, closing her eyes and crossing her fingers.

Herbie threw a switch, and the snow maker sputtered to life. Little by little, it began vacuuming up the sloshy snow, until they were standing only ankle deep in it. After about ten minutes, only a few puddles remained.

"That was genius, Herbie," Lexi said.

"It would have been genius if it worked in the first place. I suppose I'll have to go back to the ol' drawing board." He sounded sad and tired.

"We'll get some paper towels and mop up the rest of the water," Kylie assured him. "It was a good try, Herbie."

Their adviser shrugged. "Well, Rome wasn't built in a day."

Kylie shuddered. "Please don't mention Rome. We had Julius Caesar barking orders at us all afternoon."

"Delaney is on a power kick, big-time," Lexi explained to Herbie. "It's like nothing matters to her except winning the student government race at Weber Day."

"She's bossing us around," Jenna added. "And I thought my big sisters were bossy!"

"I see," Herbie said. "Have you talked to her about it? Told her how you all feel?"

"She won't listen," Kylie said. "And she's making double work for us. Now we have both her debate cupcakes and the Winter Fest cupcakes to get done."

"And no display for either of them," Lexi reminded the group.

"You leave the displays to me," Herbie said. "I can fix this—and I can come up with a real showstopper for Delaney as well."

For the first time, Kylie didn't argue with him. "Sure, Herbie. Go for it."

"Really? You're trusting him with Delaney's display?" Lexi whispered.

Kylie shrugged. "Delaney said she wants a big, flashy display."

"And a big, flashy display is what she'll get!" Herbie proclaimed, overhearing her. "That's my specialty."

Who's the Boss?

Delaney peeled back the wrapper on a cupcake from the first batch out of the oven and took a bite. Liquid oozed out of the middle. "Ick!" she cried. "It's supposed to be rich and moist, not drippy."

"They can't be *that* bad," Sophie insisted, taking a bite as well. She made a face. "Or can they?"

"Okay, let's not panic," Delaney said, pacing the floor. She had set up the twins' playpen in the kitchen, and they were now giggling happily.

"They don't even smell good." Sophie sniffed the air. "Oh, wait... I think that's Tristan's diaper..."

"We have to make this work somehow," Delaney said, ignoring her. "What would Caesar do if he were in my shoes?"

Sophie shrugged. "Order takeout?"

Delaney tried to think of all the things Mr. G had

taught her. "He would never give up. He would never abandon the fight."

She decided the best strategy was to go back to the drawing board. "I'll have to find another cupcake that has yogurt in it," she said, flipping through pages of recipes. She noticed one that Kylie had circled in bright-red pen: honey yogurt cupcakes.

"This is it!" Delaney said. "We'll do these instead."

After they had carefully blended the batter and popped the cupcakes in the oven, she raced upstairs to change her little brother's diaper.

"This has to work. It just has to," she told him.

He cooed enthusiastically.

"You think I'd make a good fifth-grade president, don't you?"

Tristan kicked his feet in the air.

"I'll take that as a yes."

As much as she hated to admit it, maybe Kylie had been right. She *should* have written a grocery list so she wouldn't forget the cream cheese. What if she had wasted all these ingredients—and all the club's money—and had no campaign cupcakes to show for it?

She put Tristan back in his playpen with his favorite

toy dinosaur just in time for the cupcakes to finish baking. Charlotte was cheerfully banging together two plastic measuring cups that Sophie had given her. "Look, Charlotte wants to be a baker too!"

When the timer dinged, Delaney took the pan out of the oven and poked a cupcake in the center with a toothpick. "They don't seem runny this time," she said. "You want to take a taste?"

"You go first," Sophie said, crossing her fingers. Delaney gently removed the wrapper and sampled a tiny bite. Then she took another, and another. "It's good! Really good!" she said. "Kylie's recipe rocks. It's light and moist and totally delish!"

Sophie sighed. "Good, because there was no way I was going to start all over again." She tried to finger comb the clumps of cake batter out of her hair. "This cupcake business is hard work. I don't think I'm cut out for it."

"It's a lot of fun when we're all working together, cranking up the music, and singing in the kitchen," Delaney explained. "And everything goes so much quicker when we form an assembly line."

"So you *do* need your club," Sophie pointed out.

Delaney considered. "Well, yeah, we're a great team. But not when Kylie is being bossy."

"You mean when *you're* being bossy—and not getting your way," Sophie added. "Just sayin'."

"I wasn't bossy…" Delaney considered. "Was I?"

"Oh, yeah." Sophie chuckled. "Big-time."

Delaney thought for a moment. "I guess I did kind of push Jenna around in the supermarket. And I did interrupt Kylie's agenda at the meeting and tell everyone they had to pay for the ingredients for my cupcakes…"

"Oh no, you didn't!" Sophie gasped. "Laney, that's awful!"

"I know, I know," she finally admitted. "And when Kylie tried to tell me that, I cut her off. I didn't want to listen."

Sophie put an arm around her friend. "I think you know what you have to do," she said. "My work here is done."

☆ ☮ ☆

After they put the finishing touches on several dozen cupcakes and Sophie went home, Delaney called Kylie to apologize.

"How's Herbie?" she asked. "Is everything okay?"

"I thought you didn't care," Kylie replied.

"I do care! I just cared about my campaign cupcakes maybe a little bit more? I'm sorry if I got carried away."

"Carried away? You were presidentially possessed!" Kylie insisted.

"I forgot one of the ingredients—the cream cheese," Delaney admitted. "So I subbed in yogurt, but the first batch was a total disaster!"

"I bet," Kylie said.

"It had to be either Greek yogurt or baby food," Delaney said. "I didn't have a choice. But I found your recipe for honey yogurt cupcakes."

"Those are *so* good," Kylie replied. "I was going to have the club bake them for the Greek folk festival in the spring."

"They are good, and if it wasn't for your recipe, I would have no cupcakes at all," Delaney continued. "I'm sorry, Kylie. I shouldn't have been such a bossy pants."

"It's okay. I forgive you," Kylie said.

"Good!" Delaney replied, relieved. "Now can I ask you a little favor?"

Kylie knew exactly what her friend was going to say before she said it: "You still need help baking two hundred cupcakes for your debate."

"No, not exactly," Delaney said. "I need help baking 152 cupcakes. Sophie and I got four dozen done before she had to go home and do her homework."

"We'll be there tomorrow, no worries," Kylie reassured her. "If we all pitch in, we'll get it done."

"What about Winter Fest—and Herbie's snow machine?" Delaney asked.

"I think he's got it under control now," Kylie said. "At least I hope so. It was more of a Slush Fest than a Winter Fest." Then she remembered how angry she had been—and what she had told Herbie to do.

"Um, Laney, I kind of said Herbie could make your display. Don't hate me!"

"Hate you? That's awesome!" Delaney said. "Can you just imagine how cool the fifth grade would think I was if I made a mountain of slush in the auditorium?"

"I wish we could come see your debate Friday," Kylie said. "But we have to set up for Winter Fest."

"I was thinking of live streaming it so thousands of viewers could tune in around the country," Delaney said.

"What?" Kylie gasped.

"JK! Just kidding! Gotcha!" Delaney laughed. It was so easy to pull Kylie's leg! "I'll hurry over to Blakely to help as soon as I put Olivia in her place."

"Deal," Kylie said. "Just remember to be your Zany Delaney self, okay? The one you posted on Instagram this morning. That's who everyone loves. The crazy girl who dances around my kitchen with fruit on her head and always makes me laugh."

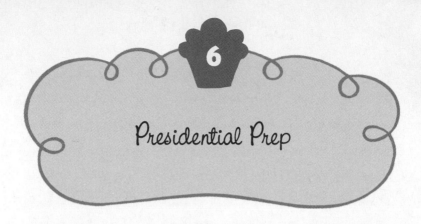

Presidential Prep

It took PLC the entire afternoon and well into the night to bake and decorate the campaign and Winter Fest cupcakes. Kylie kept them on a tight schedule, and Delaney boosted their morale whenever they complained.

"My hand is getting tired from whipping these eggs," Sadie groaned. "Can't we just make eight hundred cupcakes and call it a night?"

"Now watch me whip, whip. Now watch me bake, bake," Delaney suddenly sang while she broke into a crazy dance, spinning like a top around the kitchen. She grabbed Sadie and gave her a twirl. The other girls joined in and somehow forgot how exhausted they were—and Kylie got it all on video.

"I'm so posting this on our website," she said. "Crazy cupcake bakers in action."

When all the cupcakes were finally finished and packed

up, and the girls had all gone home, Delaney realized she didn't have a lot of time left to prepare for the debate. She raced upstairs to her bedroom and settled in at her desk, where she began outlining each of her important issues on an index card: what the problem was and how she intended to solve it.

She didn't realize what time it was until her mom poked her head in to check on her. "It's way past your bedtime, Laney," she said. "You've been awfully busy in here. Everything okay?"

Delaney nodded. "I'm just trying to make sure I know what to say when Olivia challenges me," she explained. She handed her mom a card. "Here, you pretend you're my political opponent and ask me where I stand on an issue."

Her mom sat down on the bed and read the card out loud. "Shortage of spoons in the cafeteria."

Delaney cleared her throat. "My fellow Weber Dayers, how many of you have had to eat your Jell-O with a fork? Or scoop your rice pudding with the edge of your knife? Why, I ask you? Why should we suffer with less-than-satisfactory silverware? Where are the spoons? *Where are the spoons?*"

She smiled and bowed. "How was that?"

"Impressive," her mom said.

"Okay, give me another." She handed her mom a stack of cards. "Pick a really tough one."

"Madame Candidate, where do you stand on the issue of no talking in the library?"

"Communication," Delaney began. "It is the basis of our great nation. It is the link that joins all of us together. It ends wars and keeps our relations with other foreign powers thriving. And yet in the library, Mrs. Lederman shushes us every time we even speak above a whisper! That is unfair and un-American! We need to communicate! Freedom of speech is one of our commandments!"

"I think you mean amendments—as in the Constitution," Mrs. Noonan said.

"That too!"

Her mom placed the cards on Delaney's nightstand and pulled the blanket up to tuck her in. "No more politics for tonight," she said, planting a kiss on Delaney's forehead.

"But what if I don't win?" Delaney asked.

"Then you don't. It wouldn't be the end of the world," her mom said.

"It would for me," Delaney said. "I really want this bad."

"Then try your very best. That's all you can do. And I'll

be proud of you whether you're fifth-grade president or just an average citizen."

Delaney sighed. She could just picture Olivia rubbing it in her face: "I'm better than you! I'm president...and you're not!"

She drifted off to sleep and had a bad dream. She was standing in front of the entire auditorium at the debate, dressed like a giant cupcake.

"Ha-ha!" Olivia snickered. "Zany Laney is so weird!" All her classmates—even Sophie—laughed and pointed at her.

Mr. G was there as well, looking furious. "Delaney! Haven't I taught you anything in history this year? You have to take things seriously!"

"But I did!" she cried in her dream. "I prepared and I studied and I really gave a lot of thought to what the most important issues are."

Suddenly, a shower of tater tots poured down over her head. Herbie waved from the wings of the stage. His invention was a Tot-o-Matic!

"That's what you call an important issue?" Olivia cracked up. "OMG! You are so pathetic!"

"I'm not! I wanna be president! I wanna be president!" Delaney shouted.

She woke to her mom gently shaking her. "Honey, you were having a nightmare. It's okay."

Delaney shook her head and wiped away her tears. "It's not okay," she insisted. "I just have to win the debate tomorrow. I just have to!"

Delaney could barely concentrate in fifth-period history class. The debate was next period, and she was afraid her nightmare last night was about to become reality.

"So we learned that Caesar's tragic flaws were what?" Mr. G asked the class.

Sophie raised her hand. "He was stuck up," she said. "And power hungry."

"Yes," their teacher replied. "He was ambitious and arrogant, and declared himself a dictator for life."

Delaney gulped. What if her fellow Weber Day students thought *she* was a bossy dictator? What if they hated her campaign platform and wanted to overthrow her?

"What is the difference between a dictatorship and a democracy?" Mr. G asked. He noticed Delaney in the back of the class, staring into space. "Delaney."

She snapped to attention. "What? Huh?"

"Tell me the difference between a dictatorship and a democracy."

Delaney cleared her throat. "Well, in a democracy, the leader answers to the people. He or she has to be elected fair and square, and every vote counts."

Mr. G smiled. "Excellent answer—and an excellent attitude for a presidential candidate." Just then the sixth bell rang. "Speaking of which, it's time for the fifth-grade assembly and the debate, which I will be moderating."

Delaney felt her stomach do a backflip. This was it. There was no turning back now.

"You got this," Sophie said, trying to cheer her up. "And if you need me, I'll be right there, front row."

"Thanks, Soph," Delaney replied. But she knew it would be just her and Olivia going head-to-head in the debate. No one could help her.

Face-Off

When Delaney reached the auditorium, it was packed with students and teachers. There wasn't a single seat open.

"Why is everyone here?" she whispered to Sophie.

"Um, 'cause it's an assembly and everyone *has* to be here," her friend replied. "Relax. You'll be great."

"I second that," said a voice behind her.

"And we third, fourth, and fifth it!"

It was Kylie, Lexi, Sadie, and Jenna, who had all come to support her!

"But what about the Winter Fest setup? Won't Principal Fontina be mad?" Delaney asked.

"She let us set up early so we could be here for you," Kylie said.

"And Herbie drove us all over," Sadie added. She pointed to their adviser, who was standing in the wings—just like he'd been in Delaney's dream.

"I'm so happy to see all of you," she said, hugging them. But she was a little nervous about what Herbie had up his sleeve.

"You didn't let him build a Tot-o-Matic machine, did you?" she asked Kylie quietly.

"A Tot-o-What?" Kylie giggled. "No. I checked it out before we got here, and trust me, you're gonna love your presentation, Delaney. I promise."

Delaney took a deep breath. "Okay, if you say so." She took her place onstage behind the podium next to Olivia.

"Hey, good luck," her opponent said. "I think you'd make a really great president."

Delaney was shocked that Olivia was actually being so nice.

"You too," she answered.

"And no matter who wins, we both really want great stuff for the fifth grade, right?"

Delaney nodded. "Right."

Mr. G called the assembly to attention. "Ladies and gentlemen, if you would kindly take your seats and settle down…" A hush fell over the auditorium, and Delaney could feel her palms sweating.

"Today, we have two very impressive candidates for

fifth-grade president: Delaney Noonan and Olivia Dante." The students cheered and both girls smiled nervously.

"The purpose of a debate is to hear where the candidates stand and learn their opinions on important subjects. Your job as voters is to listen carefully and form your own opinions. Who will do the best job for you and the school?"

He turned to Delaney. "The first question is about the annual fifth-grade fund-raiser. How would you raise money, and where would you suggest that money go?"

Olivia raised her hand first and spoke into the microphone at the podium. "I would do a walkathon. I would get all the fifth graders and their families on their feet—because exercise is so important to health and well-being. Then, I would use the money we raise to pay for new soccer team nets and uniforms. Our championship team deserves better. Thank you."

The Weber Day soccer team stood up and cheered. "Liv leads the way to a better Weber Day!" they shouted.

Mr. G motioned for them to take their seats. "Delaney, you're up."

Delaney looked down at her index cards, but nothing on them answered that question. She had prepared for everything from art supplies to silverware, but fund-raising? What could she say? What could she do? She had to improvise—just like she had when she forgot to buy the cream cheese for her campaign cupcakes. She looked out at Sophie and her cupcake club sitting in the first row. Sophie gave her a thumbs-up, and Kylie smiled and crossed her fingers.

Suddenly, the answer came to her. "I would do a bake sale, a huge bake sale," Delaney improvised. "I would create a campaign: Bake the Way to a Better Weber Day. And I would ask that our grade vote on the top five things we need to improve at school and put the money toward them. We should decide as a grade and not let one person make that decision."

The audience applauded enthusiastically—and Jenna whistled through her teeth. "Go, Laney! Go, Laney!" Kylie and Lexi chanted.

Mr. G held up his hand once again for silence. "Question two: The school librarian is planning to expand our book collection next year. What types of books do you think we need?"

Delaney's hand went up. There was no way Olivia was going to beat her to it this time!

"Yes, Delaney?" Mr. G said. "Your thoughts?"

Delaney froze. How was she supposed to know what books the school needed or wanted? All she could do was think of her own favorites. "I love science fiction, so I'd like to see a lot more books about aliens from outer space," she said. "And biographies of famous pop stars like Selena Gomez. I've always wanted to read about how she got into show business. Oh! Also, we could use a bunch more plays by writers like Shakespeare. He's really good!"

Mr. G smiled. "Yes, indeed he is. Olivia, your turn."

"I feel that we should focus on the classics, the greats of literature, and any books that would support our fifth-grade curriculum," she replied thoughtfully. "For example, Mr. G, you have been teaching us about Julius Caesar. More reference material on ancient Rome would be very helpful."

The audience applauded and Delaney frowned. Why hadn't *she* thought to say books about Caesar? Mr. G would have loved that!

"Those were both very good responses from our candidates," he said. "Now I'd like to turn the podium over to each of you to summarize why you think your classmates should elect you fifth-grade president. Please make your presentations."

Olivia went first. "Fifth graders, I know we like to complain a lot. We don't like this; we don't like that. Too much homework, not a long enough recess… It's really easy to say what's wrong, but it takes work and dedication to fix it. That's why I'm asking you to make me your fifth-grade president. I will work hard to find the solutions. I will take your complaints seriously, and I will bring them to the administration. I will always be willing to listen and also to be your voice. Please vote for Liv to lead the way to a better Weber Day! Thank you."

The audience clapped, and Delaney waited for Olivia to say or do something more. Her presentation had been so simple. No cupcakes, no fanfare, just solid promises to be the best leader she could be.

Mr. G looked at Delaney. "Okay, you're up," he said.

Delaney stared out at the audience staring back at her. "Hi," she began. "I, um, well, I…" She had nothing written out because there had been no time. So instead, she spoke from the heart.

"I don't have a speech," she said. A few kids laughed. "I'm just going to talk about why I want to be your president. At first, I was mad that there wasn't enough paint or costumes for the play. So I thought, let me be president and

I'll make sure I get what I want. Then, I met Liv in the hall and she was like, 'Hey, you don't even know the issues!' So, then I wanted to be president to prove her wrong." She noticed a few students in the audience frowning or rolling their eyes.

"Wait!" she pleaded. "I know that was wrong. And I learned that being president means being responsible and taking into consideration the feelings and opinions of the people who matter the most—you guys." She looked out at her PLC mates and smiled. "It's easy to let it go to your head, but I promise you this: I never will again. I don't wanna be a good president; I wanna be a *great* one. I want to be fair and I wanna be fun—'cause that's me." Herbie suddenly appeared beside her, holding a silver tray of cupcakes, each lit with a sparkler. He handed her one.

Delaney beamed. "I want to thank Herbie, my cupcake club, Sophie, and Mr. G for all your help and encouragement. I couldn't have done this without you." Then she addressed her classmates: "I want you to share your opinions and concerns with me, and I'll share my cupcakes with you!" She motioned to Kylie and company in the front row. "Guys, can you help me hand these out?"

Her friends appeared carrying cupcakes and assorted

toppings. "It's really important to me that every student's voice be heard by the Weber Day administration. You're all unique and special—which is why I want you to decorate your cupcakes exactly how you like them: sprinkles, chips, even a cherry on top. Whatever you like, your opinion counts!"

As the crowd erupted into thunderous applause, Herbie hit a button on a remote in his pocket. Suddenly, a red, white, and blue confetti cannon exploded above the stage and showered the entire auditorium. The kids went wild, and this time Mr. G didn't try to hush them.

"Well, that was definitely fun," Mr. G said, grabbing a cupcake. "And honest and heartfelt. Delaney, great job. I'm proud of you."

Olivia helped herself to a treat as well and piled on some red, white, and blue sprinkles. "Awesome," she said. "Both the cupcake and your speech."

Delaney felt like she was floating on air, just like the confetti. Even if she didn't win, she had given it her all. The only thing left to do was wait till the votes came in.

Let It Snow!

The girls all hugged Delaney and congratulated Herbie for pulling off a successful presentation.

"You actually did it, Herbie," Jenna said, patting him on the back. "Without blowing a fuse or creating *una emergencia*."

Herbie blushed. "Yes, well, it was just a question of calibrating the trigger mechanism."

Sadie chuckled. "I don't know what you're talking about, but that confetti cannon rocked. Can't wait to see what you came up with for Winter Fest."

Kylie suddenly looked at her watch. "OMG, it's three thirty! We told Principal Fontina we'd be back to hand out cupcakes at three!"

She grabbed Delaney by the arm and pulled her off the stage. "Let's go, gang. Enough politics, we've got some snow business to attend to!"

When they arrived in the gymnasium at Blakely, Principal Fontina was tapping her foot impatiently. Everyone was busy doing crafts, playing carnival games, and snacking on snow cones. They didn't seem to mind at all—but a promise was a promise and PLC was late.

"Finally!" she snapped at Kylie. "I have a huge display here covered with a drape and hundreds of hungry students waiting for cupcakes."

Herbie raced over to check the wiring one last time. "It looks good, so fingers crossed."

Kylie took a deep breath and pulled the drape off to reveal a giant snow globe filled with candy cane cupcakes. Principal Fontina handed her a microphone.

"Blakely students, if I can have your attention, please," Kylie said. All eyes turned to the center of the gym and PLC's enormous display. "In honor of the Blakely Winter Fest, Peace, Love, and Cupcakes gives you a winter wonderland!"

Herbie flipped a switch on the side of the globe, and the entire dome suddenly filled with swirling powdered sugar that settled delicately on the tops of the cupcakes. The students—and Principal Fontina—oohed and aahed.

"Herbie, you're a genius," Kylie whispered to him.

"The powdered sugar is brilliant! Now our cupcakes won't be soggy!"

"I have my moments," Herbie said with a wink.

"Thank goodness you ditched the whole idea of it snowing indoors," Lexi said. "That had disaster written all over it."

"About that," Herbie added. "I didn't ditch it entirely…"

He took the mic and faced the audience. "Ladies and gentlemen, if you will all turn your attention overhead…"

"Oh no, he didn't…" Lexi said, squeezing Kylie's hand. "I can't watch!"

Herbie hit a switch on his remote control, but nothing happened. "That's funny," he said. "It must be jammed."

"*Gracias a Dios*," Jenna said. "It doesn't work!"

"Yeah, what she said," Sadie added. "Please give it up, Herbie. We don't need another flood!"

But Herbie didn't want to give up. He kept flicking the switch on his remote while the students grew restless.

"The pressurizer must have gotten clogged," he said. "This shouldn't be happening. I tried it out, and it worked flawlessly."

Delaney saw how disappointed he was and took Kylie aside. "This means a lot to him. Can't we help?"

Kylie looked over and saw how upset their adviser was. "Guys, let's give Herbie a chance to figure it out. He didn't let us down, and we shouldn't let him down."

"I have an idea," Delaney chimed in. "We need a distraction."

She grabbed the mic out of Herbie's hand. "Hi, everyone! While we wait for our amazing, one-of-a-kind, awesome display to work, my friends from Peace, Love, and Cupcakes and I would like to entertain you with a song."

"We would?" Kylie gasped. "Laney, we don't have a song! And I don't sing!"

Delaney grabbed Lexi, who she knew had a great voice. "You're on harmony," she whispered. "Kylie, Jenna, Sadie, you guys are our backup dancers."

"What do I do?" Sadie asked in a panic.

"Sway, shimmy, bop," Delaney suggested. "I dunno. Look like you're having fun and not panicking!"

It felt good, Delaney thought, to take charge—practically presidential. She began to sing: "There's *no* business like *snow* business like *no* business I know!"

Lexi improvised the next verse: "Everything about it is so chilly…icy, slushy, slidey, and such fun!"

Then Delaney continued: "That's when I stay warm inside my kitchen, start baking cupcakes by the ton..."

Suddenly, something overhead sputtered and crackled. The lights in the gym went off, and everyone was left standing in the dark.

"Mr. Dubois!" Principal Fontina shouted. "Fix this immediately!"

"On it!" Herbie said, shining his flashlight and climbing a ladder to check the snow machine he'd mounted on the ceiling. "Gimme a sec."

There was a loud *bang*, then a *plop*, then the lights came back on. A pile of snow was now sitting on top of Principal Fontina's head and melting down her face.

"Oopsie," Herbie said apologetically. "That wasn't supposed to happen."

But before their principal could yell, small white snowflakes began delicately dancing through the air. It was beautiful...and magical. The gym was suddenly transformed into a wonderful winter wonderland.

"I said it got clogged up," Herbie called down to Kylie. "I fixed it."

"Sorry, Principal Fontina," Kylie said, handing her a napkin to wipe her face. "Herbie meant well."

"And he *did* well," Principal Fontina replied, dabbing at her nose and cheeks. "This is truly a spectacle. I've never seen anything like it."

Herbie climbed down the ladder and breathed a huge sigh of relief. "Does this mean I still have a job at Blakely?" he asked her hopefully.

The principal took a cupcake from Kylie and dug in. "Try to keep the lights on," she said with a wink and walked off to join the rest of Blakely in the fest activities.

"That was a close one!" Lexi said. "I don't wanna know what would have happened if you hadn't gotten the snow working."

Herbie shrugged. "I never doubted it for a second. Well, maybe just one second."

And the Winner Is...

Monday couldn't come soon enough for Delaney. She'd worried all weekend that no one would vote for her, even though her friends assured her she had done an amazing job at the debate.

When she got to school, there were big ballot boxes in the hallway with slips of paper next to them. Her name and Olivia's were listed on the slip, each name with a box next to it to check off. Delaney was going to put a check next to her own name, but then she hesitated. Olivia had been so nice that it was the least she could do. She voted for her and cast her ballot.

Mr. G had promised they would have the results tallied by last period and would make an announcement over the loudspeaker. Delaney anxiously stared at the clock. It was nearly three, and school was almost over for the day.

Suddenly, the speaker sprang to life. "Students, faculty,

this is Mr. Gatlin. May I please have your attention for a very important announcement."

Delaney glanced nervously at Sophie, who was seated a row behind her in math class, nibbling her nails.

Mr. G rattled off the names of the third- and fourth-grade class presidents before saying, "And this was a very interesting race for fifth grade."

What does he mean by "interesting"? Delaney thought to herself. She wished she could just hit Fast-Forward and be far, far away from this moment. It was too nerve-racking to bear!

Mr. G continued: "I would like to congratulate…"

Why was he pausing? Why couldn't he just spit it out? Didn't he know *everything* depended on his next words?

"Our new fifth-grade co–class presidents, Olivia and Delaney!"

Delaney was shocked. Co–class presidents? What did that even mean? Mr. G must have read her mind. "We had a tie between our candidates. They each had the exact same number of votes. So for the first time in Weber Day history, we are having two class presidents who will work together."

Delaney remembered how she had cast her vote for

Olivia. What if she had checked off her own name instead? Would that have made the difference and broken the tie?

"Congrats!" Sophie squealed, hugging her. "That's amazing!"

Delaney didn't know what to say. It didn't feel all that amazing. It felt like she hadn't really won—not if someone else hadn't lost.

When the end-of-day bell rang, she went to her locker to grab her jacket and bag. Everyone was patting her on the back and congratulating her. Olivia was having the same reaction at her own locker, but she snuck away to give Delaney a hug.

"I can't believe it! We *both* won," she said.

"Yeah," Delaney replied. "Cool."

Olivia looked puzzled. "You don't seem very thrilled about it. I thought you really wanted to be fifth-grade president."

"I did—and I do. But copresidents? There's no such thing. The president of the United States doesn't have a copresident."

"Oh," Olivia said. "I see. You don't wanna share the job."

Delaney realized she might have hurt Olivia's feelings. "It's not that…"

"It is," Olivia continued. "But it's a really big job, Delaney, and I'm glad I have someone like you to share it with me."

Now it was Delaney's turn to be confused. "You are?"

"Of course! You care so much about the arts, and I care so much about sports. We're the perfect team. We'll make sure it's fair for everyone."

She did have a point. What did Delaney really know about the soccer team needing uniforms or nets? And what did Olivia know about what art or drama supplies were lacking?

Mr. G found them both in the hall talking. "It's nice to see our two presidents already conferring," he said. "I hate to break this up, but Delaney has her play rehearsal after school."

With all the stress over the election, Delaney had almost forgotten she was playing Julius Caesar—and the show was less than two weeks away.

"I hope you know all your lines," Mr. G said. "I'm no Shakespeare, but I worked really hard on the script."

Delaney remembered what had made her want to run for president in the first place. "Hey, do you think we could have our first presidential meeting with the school administration tomorrow?" she asked her teacher.

"I don't see why not," Mr. G replied. "I'm sure the vice principal and the dean would be delighted to meet the new student officers."

She waited till Mr. G was down the hall to tell Olivia her plan. "I need your help," she said quietly. "We need paint and costumes for our play, and Mr. G says there's no money left in the school budget. Help me convince the administration to pay for it."

Olivia smiled. "I'd be happy to try. But what if they say no?"

Delaney raised an eyebrow. "Then I have a great backup plan."

☆ ☮ ☆

Vice Principal Ovietto and Dean Retter listened carefully the next morning as Delaney pleaded her case. "Our play looks ridiculous without the right scenery and costumes," she insisted. "Can't we just find the money somewhere?"

Dean Retter sighed. "If it were only that simple," he said. "We can't just pull funds out of thin air. They need to come from donations, allocations, fund-raising…"

"I thought you might say that," Delaney piped up.

"So I have a suggestion. We want to hold a bake sale tomorrow to pay for what we need for the play."

"We're calling it 'Sweets for Caesar,'" Olivia chimed in. "All donations will go to Mr. G's history-class play."

Vice Principal Ovietto looked concerned. "It's very short notice."

"Short notice is my specialty," Delaney insisted. "I've made three hundred cupcakes in just one night. Trust me, this is nothing out of the ordinary."

"All right," she said. "If you want to try to raise money for your play, I'm okay with it. Just save me a cupcake."

Olivia and Delaney left the vice principal's office and high-fived each other.

"Yes! We are so getting new togas," Delaney said. "Pretty white ones!"

"How are you going to make enough cupcakes to sell?" Olivia asked. "You were just making that up about three hundred cupcakes in one night, right?"

Delaney put an arm around her co–class president. "Liv, I think you need to join my PLC team after school today. We may not have uniforms, but we have aprons."

This time, Delaney made sure to write a list of ingredients and check it twice when her mom took her shopping at the supermarket. The club agreed they would donate the cost of making the cupcakes to Delaney's fund-raiser, and Jenna had come up with the two perfect flavors: Roman Ricotta Cheese Cupcakes and Brutus's Killer Carrot Cupcakes.

"I see you remembered the cheese this time," Kylie teased her as she unpacked the groceries.

"Ricotta *and* cream cheese, check-check!" Delaney said.

As the girls began dividing the ingredients into piles, preheating the oven, and firing up the mixers, Olivia looked overwhelmed.

"You guys are so professional," she said. "I can't even boil water."

"But can you crack an egg?" Sadie asked.

"I don't know," Olivia answered. "I've never tried." Sadie handed her one, and with one quick motion, Olivia cracked it open over the bowl.

"Whoa, you're a natural!" Sadie said. "And you're not bad at beating the batter either."

Olivia was having a blast, but her favorite part, by far, was delicately packing the cupcakes into the boxes so they didn't budge an inch. She made sure each box was sealed tight and tied with a pretty pink ribbon.

"I love your attention to detail," Lexi complimented her. "Usually Jenna just slaps on a bow or puts the cupcakes in backward…"

"Do not," Jenna bristled.

"Do so!" Lexi said, laughing. "I'm lucky if they're not upside down."

"The only time I put them in upside down was when they were pineapple upside-down cupcakes," Jenna replied, defending herself. "It made perfect sense."

"To you maybe," Delaney teased her. "To the rest of us they were upside down."

To further illustrate her point, Delaney did a cartwheel in the kitchen. "Look at me! I'm an upside-down cupcake!" she joked.

Olivia laughed. "Are you guys always this much fun?"

Kylie shook her head. "Nope. We're usually very serious. Delaney never puts a chocolate mustache on her face. And Jenna never accidentally dumps flour on my head."

"Wait? Is that a dare?" Jenna asked, waving a sifter in the air.

Kylie pretended to duck. "Kidding! I was kidding! No flour fights—my mom will kill us!"

After just a few hours, they had twenty dozen cupcakes baked, cooled, decorated, and packed for delivery to Weber Day. It was Lexi's idea to top them each with a laurel-leaf crown made of green fondant.

"That's so Caesar," Delaney said approvingly.

She had done a few quick calculations. They needed about $500 to purchase fabric and paints. If they sold cupcakes for $2.50 each, that meant they had to sell two hundred to meet their goal.

"I made you an extra forty—just in case," Lexi said, putting the finishing touches on the last box.

"Your club is really amazing," Olivia said. "You're so lucky to have each other."

Delaney noticed that Olivia sounded a little sad—or maybe the word was *lonely*.

"You must have tons of friends, Liv," she said. "I mean, you're so smart and involved in school stuff."

"I try to be busy," Olivia replied. "But I don't really have a lot of friends. At least not best friends like you guys are for each other. It's why I wanted to be fifth-grade president—so people would want to be my friend."

Delaney was shocked. Olivia was not at all the person she'd thought she was when they first met. She felt bad for desperately wanting to beat her. Instead, Liv was kind, considerate, and a good sport.

Delaney took Kylie aside and whispered something. Kylie nodded.

"So, Olivia, what are you doing this weekend?" Delaney asked her.

"Homework, I guess," she answered. "Why?"

"Well, we have this huge order for a sixteenth birthday party with a Hollywood theme, and the birthday girl wants a giant Hollywood sign made out of mini..."

"We could use your help," Kylie jumped in. "An extra pair of hands to help us bake and decorate and get everything packed up."

Olivia blushed. "You mean that? You're not just saying it? You want *me* to help you guys?"

Delaney remembered how great it had felt when the girls all finally accepted her as a PLC member—like she was part of a team. "We mean it," she said. "I have a lot of lines to learn for the play this weekend, so maybe you can help me with that too."

Olivia smiled. "I'd love to. Besides, what are copresidents for?"

It took Sophie, Olivia, and Delaney just a little over an hour to sell out all of their 240 cupcakes at the bake sale. Dean Retter bought the last two dozen to bring home to his wife and kids. Thanks to PLC, Mr. G was thrilled he could now have the perfect backdrops and costumes. And Delaney was equally delighted. She practiced Caesar's death scene over and over, until Mr. G told her he believed she was actually stabbed and gasping for her last breath.

"Very authentic, Delaney," he said, noting the fake blood Kylie had helped her sprinkle on her new white toga. "I especially liked the part where you clutched your throat and rolled across the stage making a gurgling noise."

Delaney remained motionless.

"Delaney?" Mr. G said, gently tapping her with his foot. "You can get up now."

Delaney leaped back up to her feet. "It's not long

enough," she said. "I think Caesar would have had a long, drawn-out death scene, don't you? At least five minutes."

Sophie shook her head. "I think the whole thing is too much. The blood? The gore? It's gross. I mean, why do we have to assassinate anyone? It's mean and violent."

"Unfortunately, it's how the senators handled their grievances with Caesar," Mr. G said.

"Well, it's icky." Sophie sighed. "If I were Brutus, I would have handled it better."

"It's history," Delaney insisted. "You can't rewrite history."

Mr. G thought for a moment. "And why couldn't we? What would you do differently, Sophie—I mean, Brutus—if your friend Caesar was out of control?"

"I'd sit him down and tell him to chill out," Sophie said. "I'd say, 'Jules, enough is enough. If you don't stop bossing everyone around, you're going to be friendless—and I'm gonna have to take daggers into my own hands.'"

Their teacher scribbled some notes on the script. "I like it. Keep going with this."

"Brutus would make Caesar see the error of his ways through peaceful negotiation," Sophie continued. "I think that would be a much better solution. And there'd be no killing involved."

"That's ridiculous! Why doesn't Brutus just take him to lunch while he's at it? Or buy him a frappuccino? That isn't how it's supposed to happen!" Delaney cried.

Sophie didn't like it one bit that her friend was dissing her ideas in front of the class and Mr. G. "Well, maybe it *would* happen that way if Caesar wasn't so obsessed with hogging the spotlight!"

A hush fell over the classroom as Sophie and Delaney stared each other down.

Mr. G tried to referee: "I think we've tossed out some good ideas here, and I welcome all students' input."

"You're being the tyrant, not me," Delaney told Sophie. "You're the one trying to get your own way. You don't even want to *try* to work this out."

"Why should I?" Sophie asked. "Face it. My idea is the better one, and you just can't handle it."

"I think we should call our play *Rome Reimagined* and show what would have happened if things had gone down differently," Mr. G said, stepping between them. "Violence is never the answer—and right now what I want is peace in this classroom. Is that clear?"

"But it's an awesome death scene!" Delaney protested. "I love my death scene."

"Well, now Brutus and Caesar can hug it out," Sophie said. "So much better!"

"Sophie, it's not *just* your opinion that counts," Delaney protested. She felt like her friend was being completely inconsiderate.

"Well, Mr. G likes it," Sophie fired back. "So that's two opinions that count."

Delaney looked to Mr. G for support, but he was too busy tearing pages out of the script—pages that she was sure included her death scene.

"It isn't fair," she said, pouting.

But Sophie wasn't interested in being fair, and that left Delaney feeling both angry and sad. Why was her friend treating her this way?

"I'll have the new scenes for you tomorrow morning," Mr. G called after them as the bell rang. "Good work today, class. I like to see you really thinking hard about how to make the play better."

Sophie ran out before Delaney could say another word.

"What's wrong?" Olivia asked, spying Delaney by her locker. "Why the long face? I thought you'd be happy with the money we raised."

"I would be," Delaney said, "but Sophie is bossing me

around and totally changing the play. She's turned a classic tragedy into *Peace, Love, and Caesar*. It's so wrong!"

Olivia couldn't help but chuckle. "It's pretty funny, don't you think?"

"No, not really," Delaney said, pouting.

"But it could be—right, Zany Laney?"

Delaney suddenly had an idea. "Liv, did I ever tell you you're a genius?" she asked, hugging her copresident. "I think I know how to make our play a huge hit—and save my death scene. It'll be so great that Sophie won't mind at all...I hope!"

☆ ☮ ☆

Delaney went along with all of the script's rewrites during rehearsals, but she was secretly planning her own revisions for the day of the play. She tried to talk to Sophie one last time before the curtain went up.

"Remember when you warned me that I was being too bossy with the cupcake club?" she asked her friend.

"Yeah, you were. So?"

"So, you made me think about it and realize I wasn't being fair. I called Kylie to say I was sorry."

Sophie adjusted her toga. "I don't get what this has to do with our play."

"Soph, you're being bossy. I get that you didn't like the way things were, but you can't just ignore what everyone else thinks and feels."

"Everyone? I don't see anyone complaining, Laney—except you," Sophie said. "You're the only one who doesn't like the new ending."

"Well, that should be enough. I'm your BFF. You should care."

Sophie shrugged. "What I care about right now is doing our show." She pulled back the curtain to reveal the audience packed with fifth-grade students and faculty. "Can we please talk about this later?"

Delaney shook her head. "Later will be too late. Please, Soph, can't we come up with a compromise? Something we could do that we would both be happy with?"

"You play your part, and I'll play mine," Sophie insisted. "Stick to the script."

"Places," Mr. G called. "It's showtime!"

"Did you hear that?" Sophie said, pushing Delaney aside to get to the stage.

Delaney raised an eyebrow. *Oh, I heard it*, she thought to herself. Loud and clear.

As Mr. G cued the lights and the curtain, Delaney

appeared onstage in her red flowing cape and laurel-leaf crown.

"I, Caesar, declare myself dictator for life!" she said, storming across the stage.

"But, Caesar, listen to your senators," Sophie said as Brutus pleaded with her.

"What?" Delaney replied. "Speak up! Can't hear ya!"

A few students chuckled as she pretended to be hard of hearing.

Sophie cleared her throat and spoke louder. "I said, 'Caesar, listen to us! We want what is best for the people.'"

"What's that?" Delaney repeated. "You want vests for the people?"

She dashed offstage and came back wearing a bright-yellow traffic vest. "Will this do? I think it also comes in blue…"

This time, the audience roared with laughter.

"Let me tell ya something, Brutus," she continued. "I know how you feel. You're so mad that you could just kill me."

Sophie shook her head. "No! No! I don't want to kill you. That would be awful."

"Even if I did this?" She took a cupcake from inside the vest pocket and smooshed it in Sophie's face.

"Delaney!" Sophie cried. "It's not funny."

"But it is!" Delaney whispered to her. "Come on, Soph, have some fun with it! You don't have to be a brutal Brutus, and I can have my death scene. We can compromise and both be happy."

Sophie looked out at the audience—they *did* seem to be enjoying themselves. Maybe Delaney's new twist wasn't such a bad idea. They both got what they wanted: a death scene minus the gore and guts.

"Okay," she whispered to Delaney. "What the heck. What do we do now?"

Delaney pulled another cupcake out of her other pocket and handed it to her. "Go ahead. Do me in!"

"Take that!" Sophie exclaimed as Brutus, smooshing the cupcake in Caesar's face. "I hereby end your reign of tyranny!"

"Yes! Finally!" Delaney cheered as she began her dramatic death dance around the stage. She teetered this way…then that way…then flopped facedown on the stage and twitched for several more minutes.

Sophie couldn't help but crack up. Only Delaney could make death a laughing matter!

"Is he gone?" another student playing a senator asked, hovering over Delaney's fallen form onstage.

"Oh, I hope so," Sophie said. "She—I mean he—was such a pain in the butt!"

With that, Mr. G lowered the curtain and the audience cheered.

"Well, that was definitely…*creative*," he told the cast. "I wasn't expecting comedy improv, but you guys did a great job. Especially you, Sophie. You made us feel Brutus's frustration…in frosting."

"Hey, isn't anyone gonna help me up?" Delaney called from her spot on the floor.

Sophie offered her a hand. "You're crazy, you know that?" she told her friend.

"I prefer Zany. It rhymes with Laney."

"I guess I should know better than to mess with history…or your monologue," Sophie said. "I guess I wasn't being a very considerate friend."

"Ya think?" Delaney said. "I tried telling you, but you wouldn't listen. This was the only way I could get through."

"I'm sorry," Sophie replied, hugging her. "You're right. I was being awful."

"Hey, it happens to the best of us," Delaney said. "But I think we both make better friends than dictators."

Olivia was the first person to greet Delaney when she came offstage. She was holding a huge bowl of Caesar salad with a bow on it.

"Bravo!" she said. "This is for the star of the show." She handed it to Delaney and waited for her reaction.

Delaney burst out laughing. Olivia was finally getting her sense of humor!

"Of course, I couldn't find any forks in the cafeteria," Olivia said, handing her a spoon. "You'll have to use this."

Delaney rolled her eyes. "I think that has to be the next thing we fix," she said. "The great silverware shortage at Weber Day."

"*We?*" Olivia pointed out. "You mean you *like* being a copresident?"

Delaney considered for a second. "Caesar might have been a solo act, but I think it's awesome sharing the job with you."

"And if there's one thing we've learned today, it's that every opinion counts," Sophie reminded her. She wiped a smudge of frosting off her cheek. "Yum, cream cheese frosting, my fave. Thanks, Laney."

"My pleasure," Delaney answered. "If I was gonna

smoosh a cupcake in my bestie's face, it would have to be her favorite flavor."

She glanced down at the bowl of salad in her hands and got that mischievous look in her eye again. "From now on, I think our motto needs to be 'lettuce' all work together."

Sophie groaned. "Ugh! I swear, I'm gonna 'kale' you both!"

But all was well in ancient Rome…and Weber Day.

Chocolate Candy Cane Cupcakes

Cupcakes

Makes 12 cupcakes

- 1 cup sugar
- ¾ cup (1½ sticks) unsalted butter, room temperature
- 3 eggs
- 1 teaspoon vanilla extract
- ¾ cup all-purpose flour
- ¾ cup unsweetened cocoa powder (I like Hershey's.)
- ½ teaspoon baking powder
- ½ teaspoon salt
- ½ cup sour cream

Directions

1. Have a grown-up help you preheat the oven to 350°F. Line a muffin pan with cupcake liners. (For a candy cane theme, I like to use red-and-white-striped ones.)

2. In the bowl of an electric mixer set on high speed, cream together the sugar and butter until light and fluffy.

3. Reduce speed to low, and beat in the eggs one at a time. Add the vanilla, and mix until combined.

4. In a separate medium-sized bowl, whisk together the flour, cocoa, baking powder, and salt.

5. Slowly add the dry ingredients into the wet mixture, alternating them with the sour cream. Beat for approximately two minutes on low to medium speed until the batter is smooth. Be careful not to overbeat.

6. Using an ice-cream scoop, spoon the batter into the cupcake liners until they are two-thirds full. Bake for 18–20 minutes, or until a toothpick inserted in the middle of a cupcake comes out clean.

7. Have an adult remove the pan from the oven, and allow the cupcakes to cool completely, about 15 minutes, before frosting.

Peppermint Buttercream Frosting

1 cup (2 sticks) unsalted butter, room temperature

3 cups confectioners' sugar

4 tablespoons whipping cream

2 teaspoons peppermint extract

3 candy canes

Directions

1. Cream the butter in the bowl of an electric mixer set on high speed.

2. Reduce the speed to low, and carefully add the confectioners' sugar and the cream and peppermint extract, alternating between them. Beat for about two minutes until the frosting is light and fluffy.

3. Use a piping bag with a tip to create your frosting. (I like to pipe mine to look like a swirl.)

4. Place the candy canes in a plastic freezer storage bag, and seal the bag.

5. Have a grown-up help you use a mallet or the back of a large serving spoon to crush the canes into tiny bits.

6. Sprinkle the candy bits over the tops of the cupcakes, and serve your sweet, minty treat!

Delaney's Campaign Cupcakes (Honey with Greek Yogurt)

Cupcakes

Makes 12 cupcakes

- ⅓ cup unsalted butter
- ½ cup honey
- 2 eggs
- ¼ cup plain Greek yogurt
- 1 teaspoon vanilla
- 1½ cup all-purpose flour
- 1 teaspoon baking powder
- ½ teaspoon baking soda
- ½ teaspoon salt

Directions

1. Have a grown-up help you preheat the oven to 350°F. Line a muffin pan with cupcake liners.
2. With a grown-up's help, heat the butter until melted in a small saucepan over medium heat.

3. In the bowl of an electric mixer set on high speed, mix together the honey and melted butter.

4. Reduce the mixer setting to low, and beat in the eggs one at a time. Add the Greek yogurt and vanilla.

5. In a separate medium-size bowl, whisk together the flour, baking powder, baking soda, and salt.

6. Slowly add the dry ingredients into the honey mixture, beating for approximately two minutes on low or medium speed until the batter is smooth.

7. Using an ice-cream scooper, spoon the batter into the cupcake liners until they are two-thirds full. Bake for 18–20 minutes, or until a toothpick inserted in the middle of a cupcake comes out clean.

8. Have an adult remove the pan from the oven, and allow the cupcakes to cool completely, about 15 minutes, before frosting.

Vanilla Buttercream Frosting

1 cup (2 sticks) unsalted butter, room temperature

3 cups confectioners' sugar

4 tablespoons whipping cream

Directions

1. Cream the butter in the bowl of an electric mixer set on high speed.

2. Reduce the speed to low, and carefully add the confectioners' sugar, alternating with the cream. Beat for about two minutes until the frosting is light and fluffy.

3. Using a piping bag or spatula, frost your cupcakes. (I like to drizzle mine with a little honey on top as well!)

Roman Ricotta Cheesecake Cupcakes

Makes 12 cupcakes

- ¾ cup graham cracker crumbs
- 2 tablespoons sugar
- 3 tablespoons butter
- 4 ounces cream cheese (½ package), softened
- ½ cup ricotta cheese
- ½ cup sugar
- 2 eggs
- ⅓ cup heavy cream

Directions

1. Have a grown-up help you preheat the oven to 325°F. Line a muffin pan with cupcake liners, and spray the liners with a nonstick cooking spray.
2. To make graham cracker crumbs, put the crackers in a plastic freezer storage bag, and seal the bag. Have a grown-up help you use a mallet or the

back of a large serving spoon to crush the crackers into crumbs.

3. In a small bowl, combine the graham cracker crumbs and sugar.

4. With a grown-up's help, heat the butter until melted in a small saucepan over medium heat. Stir the melted butter into the crumb mixture.

5. Press about a tablespoon of the crumb mixture into the bottom of each cupcake paper.

6. In the bowl of an electric mixer set at low speed, combine the cream cheese, ricotta cheese, sugar, eggs, and heavy cream. Blend until creamy.

7. Spoon the cheesecake mixture into the liners until they are two-thirds full.

8. Bake for 10–15 minutes, or until just set. Don't overbake.

9. Have an adult remove the pan from the oven, and let the cupcakes cool for 15 minutes before chilling in the fridge for at least an hour.

10. I like to top each cupcake with a dollop of whipped cream and some fruit—a strawberry, a raspberry, or a few blueberries—for that authentic cheesecake look and flavor.

Carrie's Q&A:
Letty Alvarez

LA Sweetz owner Letty Alvarez not only makes amazingly yummy cupcakes in her Florida-based bakeries, she also competed to be the Cake Boss's Next Great Baker. I asked her to dish on her biz and hanging with Buddy...

Carrie: LA Sweetz is my fave cupcakery in Miami! How and when did you start it? Was it hard to grow the business?

Letty: Thank you for that awesome compliment! My husband and I started LA Sweetz in 2008 with the last of our family's savings ($5,000). The country was going through a recession at the time. It was a huge gamble to start our business, but it was one of the best decisions I have ever made in my life. Growing the business took time, but we are happy to admit that it was not hard to grow due to the number of fans we accumulated throughout the years that fell in love with our product and our amazing customer service.

Carrie: What makes a great cupcake, and what are your fave flavors you've created? What are your most popular bestsellers?

Letty: Quality ingredients are what physically make a great-tasting cupcake, but the magic of how it is made is why I think our cupcakes are the best! From the moment you enter LA Sweetz, you are greeted with a friendly smile, loud, fun music, and a bubbly color scheme throughout the store. I truly believe what makes our cupcakes great is the amount of love that we make them with and serve them with.

Narrowing down my favorites is a difficult task since they are all so yummy, but I would say my all-time three faves are: Chocolate Raspberry, Captain Jack, and Ricky Martin! Chocolate Raspberry needs no explanation: it's a delicious chocolate cake filled with raspberry puree, topped with dark chocolate buttercream, and drizzled with raspberry syrup. Captain Jack is a chocolate, English toffee, and crushed Oreo cookie cake that's filled with caramel and topped with dark chocolate buttercream that's drizzled with caramel and topped with crushed Oreo dust. Finally, the Ricky Martin was our hit on *Cupcake Wars*. It's an adult cupcake because it is alcohol-infused. It's a coconut and rum cake topped with a sweet dulce de leche buttercream and a candied coconut crunch! Our top sellers continue to be Guava, Red Velvet, and Triple Chocolate.

Carrie: You competed on *The Next Great Baker*! What was that like? Was it hard? Scary? Is Buddy nice?

Letty: Yes! I was one of thirteen candidates selected from over 75,000 applicants to participate in Season 3 of TLC's *The Next Great Baker* with TLC's *Cake Boss* superstar Buddy Valastro. The amazing experience is one I will forever treasure. It was incredibly difficult on many levels. I had to leave my family and business for six weeks, and live alone and isolated in a hotel room. I had to first compete against strangers that eventually became like family because we only had each other while we were there.

It was mentally hard to compete with so many different types of personalities and people you knew had a better skill set than you. It was also scary because we all had different reasons to be there, causes and goals that propelled us to compete, and at the same time we started thirteen strong and week to week would lose a teammate and had to deal with the possibility that we may be the next to go. I can say Buddy was an intense person, but I truly admire his dedication to his family and his business ambition. But his piercing stares were always nerve-racking for me!

Carrie: What advice do you have for kids who want to one day own their own baking biz?

Letty: My advice to any kid or adult who wants to enter the baking business is to make sure they love what they are doing, because day in and day out of producing the same baked goods can wear you down if you don't truly love it. But if you are a person like me and you do love baking and putting smiles on people's faces, then owning your own bakery business will make you feel complete, content, and very sweet!

Carrie: What are your future plans for LA Sweetz? Did you ever think of opening in LA?

Letty: The future for LA Sweetz is very sweet, now that we have franchised. Expansion to the West Coast is very possible, but for now we are starting to plan out and grow the five stores we have sold in Orlando. Who knows? Maybe Mickey Mouse might fall in love with us as well!

Carrie: I know you're a mom! Do you teach your kids to bake? Do they help out at the bakery?

Letty: I am a mom of five! My oldest son is twenty-three, and he is my head pastry chef; my daughters, who are nineteen and sixteen, work at the shops' front counters selling cupcakes; and my twins, who are eleven now, are my best research and development specialists! They taste test everything we create and give us critical feedback with a thumbs-up or thumbs-down. Honestly, I would love for my kids to take over the business someday, but I realize LA Sweetz is my dream and I am open to them making their own way in life and choosing their own dreams to pursue. They've all had fun in the bakery baking, frosting, and creating yummy cupcakes. Only time will tell if what I am working so hard to build is something they want to inherit and run in the future. We shall see!

Acknowledgments

Many thanks to all our family and friends who make Cupcake possible:

The Kahns, Berks, and Saperstones, as always, for their love and support. Daddy and Maddie: love you to the moon and back!

Our supersweet agents, Katherine Latshaw and Frank Weimann from Folio Lit; our great team at Sourcebooks Jabberwocky: Steve Geck, Kate Prosswimmer, Alex Yeadon, Elizabeth Boyer.

Shout-out to Thommie Retter (you got a character named after you!) and all our TW2B friends and family. Love you guys!

About the Authors

Sheryl Berk is the *New York Times* bestselling coauthor of *Soul Surfer*. An entertainment editor and journalist, she has written dozens of books with celebrities, including Britney Spears, Jenna Ushkowitz, and Zendaya. Her daughter, Carrie Berk, is a renowned cupcake connoisseur and blogger (facebook.com/PLCCupcakeCLub; carriescupcakecritique .shutterfly.com; Instagram @plccupcakeclub) with over 100,000 followers at the tender young age of twelve! Carrie cooked up the idea for The Cupcake Club series while in second grade. To date, she and Sheryl have written eleven books together (with many more in the works!). *Peace, Love, and Cupcakes* had its world premiere as a delicious new musical at New York City's Vital Theatre in 2014. The Berk ladies are also hard at work on a new series, Fashion Academy, as well as its musical version—*Fashion Academy: The Musical*, which premiered in October 2015 in New York City.

Peace and Love and CUPCAKES

Meet Kylie Carson.
She's a fourth grader with a big problem. How will she make friends at her new school? Should she tell her classmates she loves monster movies? Forget it. Play the part of a turnip in the school play? Disaster! Then Kylie comes up with a delicious idea: What if she starts a cupcake club?

Soon Kylie's club is spinning out tasty treats with the help of her fellow bakers and new friends. But when Meredith tries to sabotage the girls' big cupcake party, will it be the end of the cupcake club?

Book
1

Recipe For Trouble

Meet Lexi Poole.

To Lexi, a new school year means back to baking with her BFFs in the cupcake club. But the club president, Kylie, is mixing things up by inviting new members. And Lexi is in for a not-so-sweet surprise when she is cast in the school's production of *Romeo and Juliet*. If only she could be as confident onstage as she is in the kitchen. The icing on the cake: her secret crush is playing Romeo. Sounds like a recipe for trouble!

Can the girls' friendship stand the heat, or will the cupcake club go up in smoke?

Book
2

Winner Bakes All

Meet Sadie.

When she's not mixing it up on the basketball court, she's mixing the perfect batter with her friends in the cupcake club. Sadie's definitely no stranger to competition, but the oven mitts are off when the club is chosen to appear on *Battle of the Bakers*, the ultimate cupcake competition on TV. If the girls want a taste of sweet victory, they'll have to beat the very best bakers. But the real battle happens off camera when the club's baking business starts losing money. Long recipe short, no money for icing and sprinkles means no cupcake club.

With the clock ticking and the cameras rolling, will the club and their cupcakes rise to the occasion?

Book

3

Icing on the Cake

Meet Jenna.

She's the cupcake club's official taste tester, but the past few weeks have not been so sweet. Her mom just got engaged to Leo—who Jenna is sure is not "The One"—and Peace, Love, and Cupcakes has to bake the wedding cake. Jenna is ready to throw in the towel, especially when she hears the wedding will be in Las Vegas on Easter weekend, one of the most important holidays for the club's business!

Can Jenna and her friends handle their busy orders—and the Elvis impersonators—or will they have a cupcake meltdown?

Book
4

Baby Cakes

$\mathcal{M}$eet Delaney.

New cupcake club member Delaney is shocked to find out her mom is expecting twins! When her parents first tell her, the practical joker thinks they must be pulling her leg. For ten years she's had her parents—and her room—all to herself. She LIKED being an only child. But now she's going to be a big sis.

The girls of Peace, Love, and Cupcakes get together to bake cupcakes and discover Delaney is worried about what kind of a big sister she will be. She's never even babysat before! But her cupcake club friends rally to her side for a crash course in Big Sister 101.

Book
5

Royal Icing

$\mathcal{M}$eet Kylie.

As the founder and president of Peace, Love, and Cupcakes, Kylie's kept the club going through all kinds of sticky situations. But when PLC's advisor surprises the group with an impromptu trip to London, the rest of the group jumps on board—without even asking Kylie. All of sudden, Kylie's noticing the club doesn't need their president nearly as much as they used to. To top it off, the girls get an order for two thousand cupcakes from Lady Wakefield of Wilshire herself—to be presented in the shape of the London Bridge! Talk about a royal challenge…

Can Kylie figure out her place in the club in time to prevent their London Bridge—and PLC—from falling down?

Book
6

Sugar and Spice

$\mathcal{M}$eet Lexi.

The girls of Peace, Love, and Cupcakes might be sugar and spice and everything nice, but the same can't be said for Meredith, whose favorite hobby is picking on Lexi. So when the PLC gets a cupcake order from the New England Shooting Starz—the beauty pageant Meredith is competing in—the girls have a genius idea: enter Lexi into the competition so she can show Meredith once and for all that she's no better than anyone else. Problem is, PLC has to make Lexi a pageant queen—and 1,000 cupcakes—all in a matter of weeks!

Have the girls of Peace, Love, and Cupcakes bitten off more than they can chew?

Book 7

Sweet Victory

$\mathcal{M}$eet Sadie.

MVP Sadie knows what it takes to win—both on the court and in the kitchen. But when Coach Walsh gets sick and has to temporarily leave school, Sadie's suddenly at a loss. What will she do without Coach's spot-on advice and uplifting encouragement? Luckily, Sadie's got Peace, Love, and Cupcakes on her side. Her friends know that the power of friendship—and cupcakes—might be just what Sadie needs! Together, they rally to whip up the largest batch of sweet treats they've ever made, all to help support Coach Walsh. When the going gets tough, a little PLC goes a long way. But this record-breaking order might just be too much for the club…

Can the girls pull it together in time to score a win for Sadie—and Coach Walsh?

Book
8

Bakers on Board

$\mathcal{M}$eet Jenna.

It's "anchors aweigh!" for the Cupcake Club!

Jenna's stepdad, Leo, is taking his family on a Caribbean cruise. Unfortunately, Jenna's younger siblings get the chicken pox, leaving Leo with four extra tickets. Enter Peace, Love, and Cupcakes! Leo says Jenna's four besties can come—in exchange for baking twelve thousand cupcakes for his company's pirate-themed event. Shiver me timbers, that's a lot of icing! Now pros the cupcake-baking game, PLC takes on the challenge.

But when a freak rainstorm flares up on the night of the big event, will it be rough seas for the girls?

Book
9